Copyright © 2021 Clavis Publishing Inc., New York

Visit us on the Web at www.clavis-publishing.com.

Beaver Doesn't Open the Door written by Shuo Pang and illustrated by Ziying Jiang

ISBN 978-1-60537-648-6

This book was printed in May 2021 at Nikara, M. R. Štefánika 858/25, 963 01 Krupina, Slovakia.

First Edition
10 9 8 7 6 5 4 3 2 1

Written by Shuo Pang
Illustrated by Ziying Jiang

Beaver
Doesn't Open
the Door

Clavis

NEW YORK

"A-achoo." Beaver sneezes and snorts all the time
for some unknown reason. He's miserable!
Tissue after tissue, handkerchief after handkerchief,
his poor nose is as big and red as a clown's.

"I might have a cold." Beaver takes some medicine and sleeps drowsily for the whole afternoon.

"Ahem, ahem, ahem," Beaver coughs, waking up worse than ever.

Not only does he not feel like eating, but he also has a headache. He feels hot all over and he coughs violently.

"Oh, no! I won't catch the latest virus, will I?" Beaver feels a little uncomfortable, as if there are butterflies in his stomach. "According to the news, the typical symptoms of this virus are cough and fever!" Beaver quickly finds the thermometer and tucks it carefully under his armpit. A few minutes later, the thermometer jumps to *102°!*

Just then, there's a knock on the door and Mrs. Swan, the neighbor, comes by.

Beaver thinks for a moment. Then he shouts out the door, "Mrs. Swan, I've got a fever and a cough. Perhaps I've caught the latest virus . . . *for your safety,* **I can't open the door."**
"I came to check on you because I heard your cough," Mrs. Swan replies. "Don't worry, I'll call the doctor for you."

Just as Mrs. Swan leaves, another neighbor knocks on the door. "Are you all right, Beaver?" asks Aunt Mole. She heard Beaver cough and brought a bowl of soup. "Thank you for your kindness, Aunt Mole, but I may have caught a virus, and *for your safety,* **I can't open the door,"** says Beaver shyly.

Miss Raccoon brings Beaver
a bunch of small daisies.
Apologetically, Beaver says,
"Thank you for your kindness,
Miss Raccoon, but I may have
caught a virus, and *for your safety,*
I can't open the door."

Grandma Antelope brings Beaver a scarf, but Beaver refuses again. "Thank you, Grandma Antelope, I really appreciate your kindness, but I may have caught a virus, and *for your safety,* **I can't open the door."**

It isn't until Doctor Rhinoceros and Nurse Ostrich arrive that Beaver opens the door. All three of them are wearing a mask to better protect themselves from the virus.

The news that Beaver might be infected spreads like the wind through every house in Warm Community. His neighbors are worried about him.

It's essential that all the neighbors stay home now. That way, the virus can't spread any further.

If they do leave their houses, it's important that the neighbors wear masks, just like Doctor Rhinoceros and Nurse Ostrich.

They must also keep their distance at all times.

And they shouldn't forget to thoroughly wash or disinfect their hands multiple times a day!

Mrs. Sika Deer quickly prints out pamphlets on the prevention of contagious diseases and brings them to the residents.

Fortunately, upon examination, it turns out
that Beaver only has a common cold and
hasn't caught the latest virus. *The residents of
Warm Community breathe a sigh of relief!*

The next day, the neighbors come to see Beaver again. Strangely, Beaver still doesn't open the door.

"Even if it's a cold, *for your safety,*
I can't open the door.
But I'll be better soon.
See you then, dear friends!"

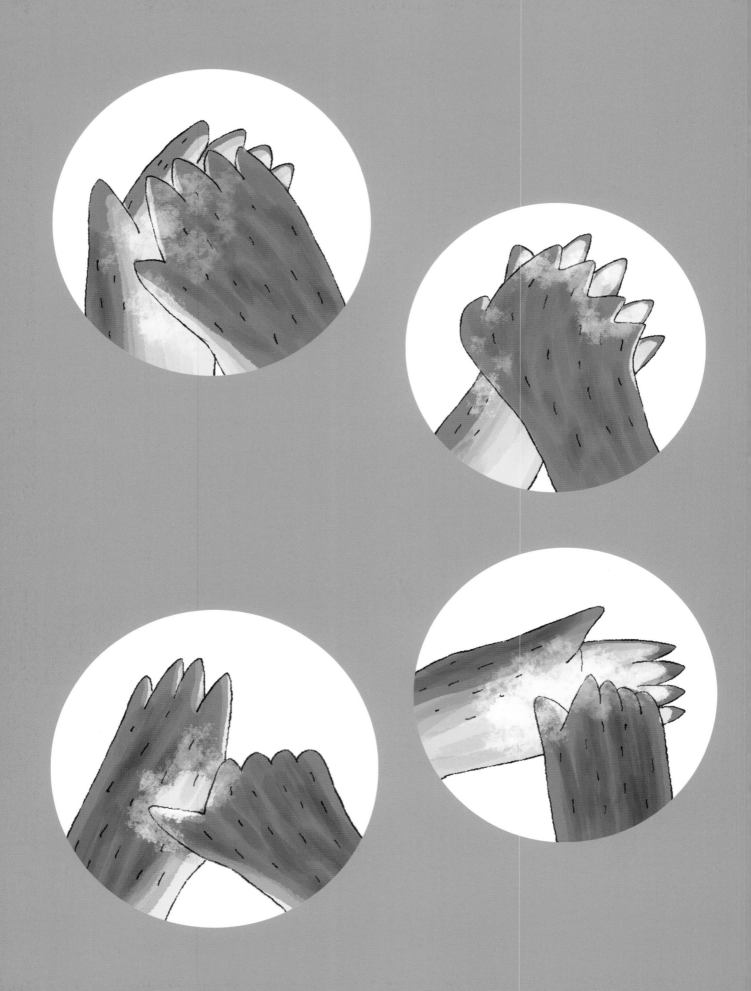